Katie's Wish

Barbara Shook Hazen

illustrated by Emily Arnold McCully

Dial Books for Young Readers  New York

To Katie, with loving wishes, and in memory of Mary Louise
B. S. H.

Published by Dial Books for Young Readers
A division of Penguin Putnam Inc.
345 Hudson Street
New York, New York 10014
Text copyright © 2002 by Barbara Shook Hazen
Illustrations copyright © 2002 by Emily Arnold McCully
All rights reserved
Typography by Atha Tehon
Text set in Minister
Printed in Hong Kong on acid-free paper
1 3 5 7 9 10 8 6 4 2

Library of Congress Cataloging-in-Publication Data
Hazen, Barbara Shook.
Katie's wish / Barbara Shook Hazen ;
illustrated by Emily Arnold McCully.
p.   cm.
Summary: Soon after Katie wishes for her potatoes to disappear during supper,
a potato famine ravages her native Ireland, forcing her to leave for America.
ISBN 0-8037-2478-0
1. Ireland—History—Famine, 1845–1852—Juvenile fiction.
[1. Ireland—History—Famine, 1845–1852—Fiction.
2. Famines—Ireland—Fiction. 3. Emigration and immigration—Fiction.]
I. McCully, Emily Arnold, ill. II. Title.
PZ7.H314975 Kat 2002
[E]—dc21   2001028254

The artwork was rendered in watercolor on Arches paper.

↣❈ *Author's Note* ❈↢

The potato famine, also known as "The Great Hunger," was the biggest tragedy and turning point in Irish history. It was a time of chaos and courage that forever changed the face of Ireland, and of America.

Between 1845 and 1850 well over one million people—approximately a fifth of the Irish population—died of starvation and contagious diseases such as cholera and typhus, which spread like wildfire. During the same time, another million left their homeland, the majority for the East Coast of America. (In just one famine year, the population of Boston, Massachusetts, increased by a third.)

What made the potato crop failure such a disaster? The almost complete dependency on this one easy-to-grow food. Most families ate little else. An average man consumed between seven and fifteen pounds a day! The pigs and the grain went to the English landowner.

What made matters worse? Unusually cold weather, plus a long history of bitter disputes and bad feeling. The English not only owned the land but passed harsh anti-Irish and anti-Catholic laws. Irish Catholics could not hold political office. Their children could not go to school. Reading and writing was taught by a hedgemaster, a traveling teacher who visited families only in the fall. It was an unfair system in which the English prospered while the Irish were put down.

What happened after the famine? Those who stayed worked to change the system. And those who left, after initial hardships, greatly enriched their new homelands. Today, wherever they are, the Irish are a proud and prosperous people.

Everyone sat Sunday-still as Grand Da said grace. "We ask God's blessing on these fields, this family, and the food we eat."

"Except the potatoes," Katie muttered under her breath. "I wish they'd go away."

They were plain-boiled and boring, not the way she liked, the way Mam used to make them, with lashings of milk, onion bits, and a knob of butter.

Uncle Eamon and Auntie Angelica gasped. Katie's older cousin, Brian, snickered. The two families always shared the after-church meal.

"Child, be careful the way you speak," Grannie chided. "Words have wings and the wee folk have ears."

"Aye," Grand Da said. "'Tis the plenty of plain pratties that fills our stomachs. Be grateful for what you've got."

"I'm sorry," said Katie, shamed. Ever since Mam died and her da left for America, she was always saying the wrong thing.

After supper, while the others chatted, Katie fed Pig the potato peelings.

She heard Grand Da's voice soar above the others. "And now her da wants Katie to come over," he was saying. "Him with his itch for roaming and big words about a better life. That's why he's sending the money—for the lass, just for the lass. Myself, I will never leave Ireland, nor will I let Katie."

Katie winced. She pulled a worn letter out of her pocket and showed Pig the words she knew by heart.

> *Dear Katie,*
> *I am in Boston Town, with Auntie Meg. America is a fine place,*
> *a land of promise. Here, schooling is in a building, not just when*
> *the hedgemaster comes. I will send for you soon.*

Soon. Katie tasted the word. It sounded as far away as Mam in heaven. Or Da in America.

"Ah, would you be missing your mother?" Grand Da asked later, on their walk through the fields.

"Aye," Katie answered.

"We've a pretty good life, don't we, now?" he said with a squeeze. "We've stories to spin, songs to sing, and a fine fat porker."

Katie wanted to say: *I miss me da too, something fierce. It's been two Christmases since he left.* But she knew Grand Da didn't want to hear that.

"Hello and good day!" a voice called out of the fog. The voice belonged to their English landlord, who owned the fields that Katie's family farmed. He was out for a ride with his son Colin.

Katie waved at Colin, who often brought her oatcakes and sometimes stayed to play. Grand Da stiffened.

Katie saw the set of his face. "Are the English all bad?" she asked, after Colin and his father passed.

"They've no use for Ireland, except to line their own pockets," Grand Da said, spitting out the words. "We break our backs working the land, but it isn't ours, not an inch!"

Grand Da calmed himself, and added, "They're not all bad. There's good and bad in every kind. 'Tis the system that's bad. But enough of troubles. Come, let us look for a fairy ring. That is a fine thing to do on a misty, moist day."

It happened overnight. One day the potatoes were firm and fine. The next they were mushy and covered with black spots.

Katie went with Grand Da and Brian to inspect them.

"There's rot everywhere," Brian said, holding up a spoiled potato. "I've never seen the likes of it. We've no food but the pratties. What can we do?"

Grand Da tasted a potato, gagged, and spit out the pieces. "We must pray tomorrow will be better," he said. "And eat what we have stored."

Katie swallowed hard. A fearful thought sank like a stone in her stomach. *It's all my fault. I wished the potatoes away.*

But tomorrow was not better. The potato rot spread quickly through the
countryside. By late summer, once-fertile fields were wasteland. Katie's grand-
parents found it harder and harder to feed the family and pay the rent money.

Grannie prayed and Grand Da blamed the English for everything, even the
worse-than-usual weather. Katie tried to be extra good. She gathered berries
and grass to stretch their meager meals.

"There is fearful famine," Brian told Grand Da one day after a trek to
town. "I've seen bloated bellies and babies too weak to blink. And a strange
fever is turning people's tongues black."

"It's a powerful sad time," Grand Da said, with a worried look at Katie.

The next day Grand Da called to Katie, "Come, lass. We've a not-so-fat pig to trot to market."

"No!" Katie shrieked.

"Aye," Grand Da said. "How can we feed a pig when we can scarce feed ourselves?"

Katie bit her lip to keep from crying. Pig was her friend. The awful all-my-fault feeling grew.

In town Katie saw children begging and overheard talk of houses tumbled and families turned out in the cold.

A man from Skibbereen told Grand Da, "In my village you can scarce tell the living from the dead. I'm thinking a curse has been laid on Ireland."

Grand Da shuddered and clasped the man's arm.

Pig sold for less than Grand Da had hoped. "I'm sorry," Katie mumbled guiltily as Pig was led away.

"So am I," said Grand Da, which made her feel worse.

On the way home they ran into Father O'Malley. "Finally, some good news," he told them. "The Americans are sending shiploads of corn, and the charity funds are growing."

"It's like spitting on a house to put out the fire!" Grand Da boomed, his voice tight with anger.

Father O'Malley then bent to Katie, who usually greeted him with a happy hug. "Why so quiet, lass?" he asked. "Where is your smile? There's still sun in the day and a song in the lark."

Katie tried to hide behind Grand Da. Father O'Malley was a man of God. She feared he could see her dark secret.

The priest gave Katie a small bag of sweets. Down the road she gave it to a beggar.

Grannie had a saying: *Troubles never come single*. It seemed all too true. In early spring Grand Da got an eviction notice from the landlord, demanding that they leave their cottage by the end of the month.

Then Grannie took sick. She lay hollow-cheeked and barely able to sup.

Grand Da made nettle tea. Katie put cold wet rags on Grannie's forehead and sobbed, "I'm sorry." Fear hugged her like ground fog.

When Grannie stopped eating, Grand Da raced to fetch Father O'Malley.

The good priest came quickly. He said prayers and heard Grannie's raspy confession. Then he turned to Katie and asked, "What are you thinking, child? You've a face as long as the river Shannon."

Katie squirmed and mumbled, "Nothing."

"Tend to your grannie and pray to God," Father O'Malley said. "You are a good, caring child."

"No, I'm not!" Katie blurted out, fists clenched.

"Aye, and take a wee nap," Father O'Malley added.

Gradually Grannie did get better.

As soon as she was out of bed, Grand Da gathered the family together. "I've thought long and come to a hard conclusion," he said. "Grannie and I will move in with Eamon's family, and I will look for road work. I am still strong and able."

"What about me?" Katie asked in a wobbly voice.

"You must go to America," Grand Da said. "Brian is big enough now to take you. These terrible times have changed my mind. It is right you be with your da, in the hope of a better future."

"Jakers!" Brian shouted. "It's what I've been wanting. And I promise to take fine care of Katie. But, Grand Da, it's a long road on an empty pocket. We've no ticket money."

"I've never touched what Katie's da sent for the boat passage." Grand Da pulled out a pouch and jingled it. "Our parting was bitter. I was dead set against his leaving. Now I know it was for the best."

Katie stared into the turf fire, her thoughts too stoppered up for words. She ached to be with her da again. But to be sent away poked holes in her heart.

Katie and Brian left a fortnight later, after hugs, good-byes, and last bowls of stirabout. Katie wore Mam's shawl. She clutched a small bundle, with a book the hedgemaster gave her, her peggy-stick doll, a bag of oatcakes, and a lump of coal for luck.

The road to Galway was rough, the walking weary. Rain soaked Katie's and Brian's clothes. Mud sucked at their shoes. Brian got occasional cart rides for Katie and tried to shield her from the most heart-scalding sights of famine and sickness.

At night they slept curled like hedgehogs in roadside ditches. To eat they scoured the woods for cress, curly dock, and berries.

Sometimes they begged. Brian sang out:

> *Sorrow and rot.*
> *Supper we've not.*
> *Please put a ha'penny*
> *In me pot.*

The pot was Brian's cap, which Katie held. One woman called his voice "sweet as a chapel bell." She gave a whole bob and a hunk of bread.

In Galway at last, they trudged to the ship's ticket office.
The next day they sailed with the tide. They were herded up the
gangplank in a push of people so fierce that Mam's shawl was
almost wrenched from Katie's shoulders.

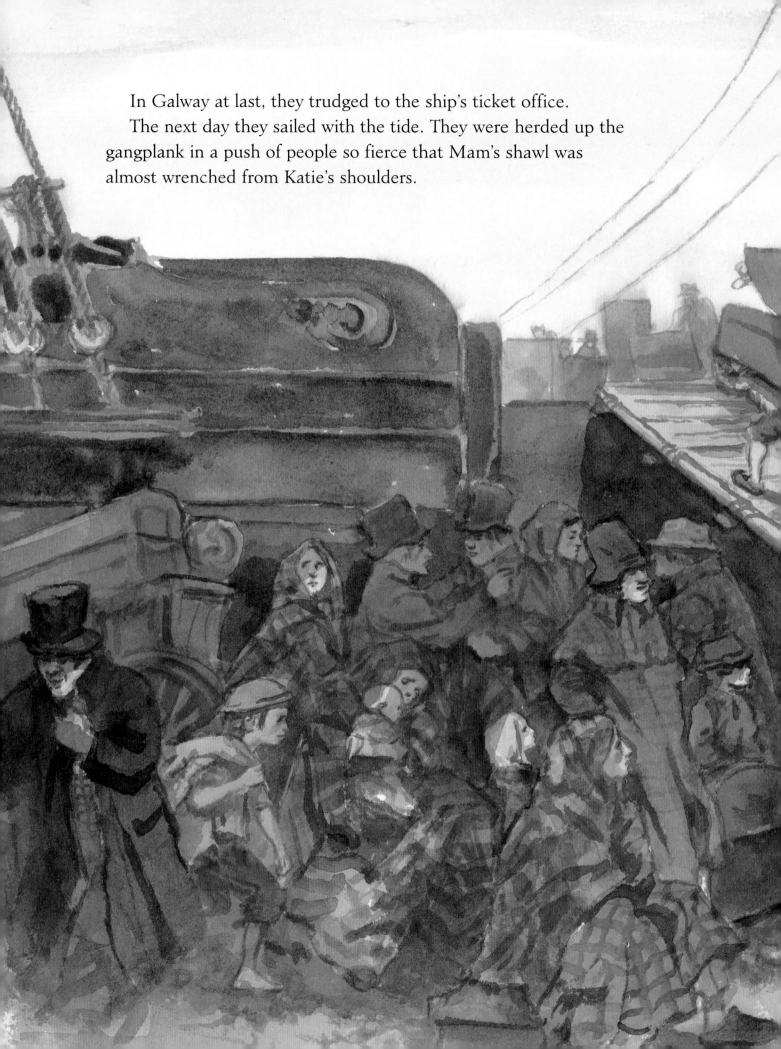

Their quarters were cramped and smelly. People moaned, and fought for blanket space. Katie hugged her knees and tried not to cry.

The trip seemed to take forever. Katie sat outside as much as possible. She clutched her doll and tried to remember Mam's arms and face, and Grand Da, so full of fun before he said the shameful thing that made the potatoes go away.

When hunger gnawed, she rocked herself to sleep, to the lullaby her mother crooned when she was little.

> *Your mam's a potato.*
> *Your da is a song.*
> *Sleep deep, sweet Katie,*
> *Though the night be long.*
> *Though rain pecks the roof*
> *And the wind howls wild,*
> *God keep you from harm,*
> *Beloved child.*

One night there was a terrible storm. Katie's stomach lurched with the waves.

"It's a nor'easter," a kind woman said. She held Katie's head and comforted her. "Such a storm means land is near. Keep hope in your heart; I hear Boston streets are paved with gold."

"That's not what I hear!" Brian, who'd been talking to the big boyos, cut in. "I hear the streets are cobblestones and the Irish are called names."

"Hush!" The woman waggled a finger and Katie covered her ears.

Brian snorted. "That's not hard in this coffin ship, with so many sick and dying."

The next day the sea quieted, a gull landed on the ship, and Katie saw shoreline. She poked Brian and shouted, "Land! I'll be seeing Da soon."

Then a new fear stabbed. *What if Da isn't there? Or doesn't recognize me so scrawny? Or doesn't want me, once he knows what I've done?*

But there he was, the same broad-shouldered, big-grinning, bear-hugging Da.

Katie flew to him and melted in his hug.

"Och, child! You're stick thin!" he said, plucking her up. "But I'd know you anywhere. And can this be Brian, a mere lad when I left, now almost a man? I want to thank you for caring for me daughter."

"Are Boston streets truly paved with gold?" Katie asked, remembering what the boat woman told her.

"Nay," said Da with a wink. "But I earn dollars on the docks where I work. I'll show you on the way home."

Home was a walk-up apartment shared with Auntie Meg's big bustling family. Auntie Meg was Mam's sister and a lot like her.

The newcomers were greeted with a barrage of questions. "Is the hunger as bad as we hear?" "How's Grannie?" "How's Grand Da?" "Do you like stickball?"

"Supper now, talk later," Auntie Meg said, steering everyone into the kitchen.

Katie slipped into a seat. The sight of all that food turned her legs to water.

Da said, "God bless those we love in Ireland and our new land, and bless the food we eat." He paused and added, "Thanks be for the bravery of Brian and the spunk of me Katie. I am full to bursting proud!"

Katie did not budge. Her eyes were fixed on the mountain of mashed potatoes with onion bits, lashings of milk, and a knob of butter, just the way Mam used to make them.

"Child, you're not eating," Da said, concerned. "Is the food not to your liking?"

"Aye, 'tis much to my liking," Katie answered. "But I can't eat."

"Why?" Da asked.

"Because I don't deserve to, because of the wicked thing I said," Katie confessed. Then, in a tumble of tears, she told of the long-ago Sunday when she wished the potatoes away, and how everything awful happened after—how "the pratties got mushy and Grannie got sick, and Grand Da was so mad he sent me away."

"Nay," Katie's da said, holding her heart-close. "Believe me, your words weren't wicked. Nor can words make bad things happen. None of it was of your doing. The famine was caused by a fungus. The fever, by disease. And Grand Da isn't mad at you. He never was.

"So eat, Katie lass, and know how big you are loved."

Katie wiped her eyes and took a bite. It was powerful good. The relief she felt, knowing what happened wasn't her fault, was like sun after rain. It filled her with warm.